OTHER YEARLING BOOKS YOU WILL ENJOY:

THE CASE OF THE DIRTY BIRD, *Gary Paulsen*
DUNC'S DOLL, *Gary Paulsen*
CULPEPPER'S CANNON, *Gary Paulsen*
THE VOYAGE OF THE FROG, *Gary Paulsen*
HOW TO EAT FRIED WORMS, *Thomas Rockwell*
HOW TO FIGHT A GIRL, *Thomas Rockwell*
HOW TO GET FABULOUSLY RICH, *Thomas Rockwell*
THE BOY WHO OWNED THE SCHOOL, *Gary Paulsen*
IT'S A WEIRD, WEIRD SCHOOL, *Stephen Mooser*
THE HITCHHIKING VAMPIRE, *Stephen Mooser*

YEARLING BOOKS/YOUNG YEARLINGS/YEARLING CLASSICS are designed especially to entertain and enlighten young people. Patricia Reilly Giff, consultant to this series, received her bachelor's degree from Marymount College and a master's degree in history from St. John's University. She holds a Professional Diploma in Reading and a Doctorate of Humane Letters from Hofstra University. She was a teacher and reading consultant for many years, and is the author of numerous books for young readers.

For a complete listing of all Yearling titles,
write to Dell Readers Service,
P.O. Box 1045, South Holland, IL 60473.

Gary Paulsen

Dunc Gets Tweaked

A YEARLING BOOK

Published by
Dell Publishing
a division of
Bantam Doubleday Dell Publishing Group, Inc.
666 Fifth Avenue
New York, New York 10103

ISBN: 0-440-40642-0

Printed in the United States of America

September 1992

10 9 8 7 6 5 4 3 2 1

OPM

Chapter 1

Duncan—Dunc—Culpepper stood next to the starting gate of the track at the Speedway Skateboarding Park. He was watching his best friend, Amos Binder, put his crash helmet on. Amos was getting ready to compete in the Skateboard National Open, amateur division.

"Are you sure you want to do this, Amos?"

"It's not a question of wanting to or not wanting to. I have to."

"I'm not real clear on this 'have to' stuff," Dunc said. "Maybe you better explain it to me again."

Amos had his helmet on and was pulling up his kneepads. "It's easy. All I have to do is win this championship."

"And?"

"And Melissa will be so impressed she'll be crazy about me forever." Amos was madly in love with Melissa Hansen. Melissa Hansen didn't know that Amos existed.

"But you've never skateboarded before in your life."

"Yes, I have."

"That driveway thing doesn't count." Amos had borrowed the neighbor's skateboard once and tried riding it down the driveway. He did fine until he reached the street. The skateboard flew out from under his feet right into the window of a passing car.

"Poor Mrs. Watkins," Amos said. "That skateboard passed right in front of her face. One of the wheels left a track on her nose."

"She went to the newspaper with a story about a UFO."

"I know. She was so frightened, she drove her car right into the living-room window of Mr. Meany."

"The policeman," Dunc said.

"Yeah." Amos picked up his board and spun all four of its wheels. "He told me that as soon as I'm old enough, he's going to put me in prison for life."

"At least there you won't get in trouble."

"I don't get in trouble now. You get me in trouble."

"I didn't have anything to do with the skateboard incident."

"And you won't have anything to do with this skateboard incident, either. For once, I'm not going to listen to any of your advice."

"But you have to get advice from someone."

"Then I'll get it from somebody else."

"Who—Lash?"

"Yeah." Lash Malesky was Amos's first cousin. He was a professional from San Diego and one of the best skateboarders in the country.

"He'll tell you the same thing I tried to," Dunc said. "He'll tell you you're crazy to try this."

"He already told me that. When I

wouldn't listen, he gave in and promised to tell me how to win." He turned his head, and together he and Dunc watched one of the other competitors wait in the starting gate.

"Now making his run," the announcer said over the loudspeaker, *"Billy Slide."*

The whistle blew and the gate opened and Billy zipped out onto the track. He went down the course flipping up in the air doing somersaults. Right before the end, he pressed into a handstand. The crowd cheered.

"Even with Lash's advice, you won't be able to do that," Dunc said.

"Except for the handstands I will."

"How do you know that?"

"I have a secret weapon."

"A secret weapon? What is it?"

"I can't tell you. It's a secret." Amos smiled the way he did when he knew something that no one else knew. He cradled the board in his arms and waited for his turn.

"Hey, dudes." They turned around. Lash was standing behind them, bobbing his head up and down and smiling. He was wearing a fluorescent orange crash helmet and a pair of reflective sunglasses. He had a board in his hand with the word *Maggie* painted across the top of it.

"Hi, Lash," Amos said. "Are you here to wish me luck?"

"Forget the luck," Dunc said. "You better just give him some advice."

"Radical," Lash said. "Cut loose and bone out all your tricks. Rock and roll on all your axle grinds. Dig into a mctwist on this jam with a five-forty—so radical. Just totally insane." He smiled and bobbed his head up and down again. Amos and Dunc looked at each other.

"Uh, thanks, Lash," Amos said.

Lash nodded. He patted Amos on the back and walked away, still bobbing his head. Amos and Dunc watched him go.

"Did you understand a word he said?" Dunc asked.

"No. I guess that's what happens when you grow up in San Diego."

"Too much sun."

"Yeah." Amos spun the skateboard's

wheels again. "So much for advice. At least I have my secret weapon."

"And what's that?"

"I can't tell you."

"Come on, Amos. I'm your best friend."

"So? Every time I tell you a secret, something bad happens."

"That isn't true."

"Oh yeah? Remember the time I told you the secret about keeping the pet bat in my bedroom closet? That wasn't good."

"But it wasn't my fault. I didn't tell your mother a thing about it."

"But she still found out. I lost a lamp, a mirror, and a bookshelf, and I got a pretty nasty bruise on my forehead."

"And she broke the tennis racket. Remember?"

"I remember. She swung that thing like she was competing in Wimbledon, and the bat still got away."

"But it wasn't my fault," Dunc repeated.

"It doesn't make any difference. Something bad always happens when I tell you secrets."

"Come on, Amos."

Amos sighed. "All right. What was my biggest problem the last time I tried to skateboard?"

"Mr. Meany."

"Besides him."

"The fact that you're such a klutz."

"No. The biggest problem was, I couldn't stay on the board. That's where the secret weapon comes in. With it, I know I can do anything any other skateboarder can do, including Lash."

"And what's your secret weapon?"

"This." He took a small plastic bottle out of his pocket.

"What's that?"

"Epoxy glue." He set the skateboard on the ground and put a couple drops of glue on it.

"Don't do this, Amos," Dunc said. "You'll kill yourself."

"No, I won't."

Dunc had to think fast. "Maybe you better just go home. What if Melissa calls and you're not there?"

"I'm having all my calls transferred to the park. If she phones me, it'll ring here."

He put two more big drops of glue on the board and stood on it. He tried to pick up his feet. They wouldn't come loose.

"Push me over to the gate."

Dunc sighed and did as he was told.

"Now competing," the loudspeaker said, *"Amos Bender."*

"That's Binder," Amos shouted. "Did you hear me? That's Bi—"

The whistle blew and the gate opened and Amos was on the track.

He swayed from side to side, barely staying upright, and his shirt flapped in the breeze behind him like a whip. He smoked up one side of the track, did a flip, and came down the other.

Dunc didn't know if it was intentional or not, but it didn't matter. The crowd and the announcer loved it. It looked like Amos might actually make it to the end of the track without requiring any major surgery when the worst possible thing in the world that could happen happened.

The phone on the judges' table rang.

Amos forgot about doing flips. He forgot about doing tricks of any kind. He forgot his name. He leveled out the board and headed straight for the table, gaining speed all the way.

He was going well over fifty when he hit the rise at the end of the track right in front of the judges.

The board flew high up in the air, but he managed to reach down and grab the receiver as he arrowed straight toward a large tree.

The phone cord had ripped off the telephone, but Amos didn't know that. A branch hit him across the stomach. He was moving so fast, he tore it off the tree right at the trunk. The branch tipped up in the air and took out three power lines as Amos landed with a crash in the parking lot.

The crowd was silent.

The loudspeaker was dead. The next contestant tried to start his run, but the electric gate wouldn't open.

"Amos, are you all right?" Dunc ran down the length of the track to the parking lot.

There was no answer. Amos was lying in the branches with the receiver up to his ear.

His feet stuck up in the air, and the wheels of the skateboard spun crazily. A squirrel sat next to his head and chattered at him angrily.

"Amos," Dunc repeated, "are you all right?"

"Hello? Hello?" Amos put the receiver down and looked up at Dunc with a disappointed expression.

"She hung up," he said.

Chapter · 2

Dunc was at Amos's house the next morning. Amos was stretched across an easy chair, and Dunc was sitting on the couch.

"I don't know if I can make it, Dunc." Amos groaned and held the four-inch-wide bruise from the branch. It went all the way across his stomach.

"You don't have to compete. They disqualified you for tearing down the power lines."

"Then why do I have to go at all?"

"Because it's your duty. The tournament had to be postponed a day because of the power loss. You have to go. You owe them at least that much."

"That's not a good enough reason."

"Then go because Lash is making his run today."

"That's not a good enough reason, either."

"I don't know what to say, then." He sat watching Amos.

"Amos?" Amos's mother called from the kitchen. She had a high voice that sometimes set Amos's back teeth on edge.

"What?"

"You can't sit in that chair all day. Your uncle Alfred is coming over to watch a football game with your father, and you know how he likes to sit in that chair."

"Uncle Alfred, Mom? Does he have to? He picks his feet."

"Everyone has little faults, son."

"It's not a little fault. His feet smell terrible."

"Well, at least he leaves his socks on. He doesn't get it all over the chair."

Amos sighed and stood slowly. "Let's go to the skateboard park."

"Are you sure you're up to it?"

"I'm up to anything if it means avoiding Uncle Alfred." He stretched out his stomach and winced.

When Dunc stood up, a growl-whimper came from behind the couch.

"What's that?"

"That's Scruff." Scruff was the family collie.

"What's he doing behind the couch?"

"I was in the bathroom this morning practicing shaving—"

"Practicing shaving?"

"You know, for when I get older. My face was all lathered up, and I had just turned on Dad's portable electric razor when I heard Melissa's ring."

"How did you know it was her?"

"I figured she'd be calling since she couldn't get me yesterday at the tournament. She has a very distinctive ring. So my older sister was sitting at the dining-room table studying infectious diseases for health class. She saw me running out of the bathroom and thought I was foaming at the mouth with rabies. She told Scruff to attack me."

"Your own dog attacks you?" Dunc stared at Amos.

"Not usually. Most of the time whenever he's near me, he just pulls his lip back and growls a little."

"He never has liked you too much, has he?"

"Not since you made me try to screw antlers on his head for that most-unusual-pet contest when we were kids."

"That almost worked. We would have won if he hadn't lifted his leg on that poodle. Reindeer don't lift their legs."

Amos smiled, remembering, then shook his head. "Anyway, just as he jumped, I backed up and tripped and the razor caught his muzzle and shaved him all the way down the belly."

"So why is he hiding?"

"He's embarrassed—he think's he's ugly. Whenever I'm in the house, he growls from behind the couch and won't come out. And I never did get to the phone. My sister answered it, but she said it was just a magazine salesperson. She's lying."

"How do you know that?"

"She lies all the time. And besides, like I said, I know Melissa's ring."

They went out the door to their bikes.

Chapter · 3

The power line was repaired at the track, and a large crowd had gathered to watch the professional competition. The bleachers were already full, so Dunc and Amos stood by the judges' table to watch. They saw Lash by the starting gate and waved. He waved back.

As they waited, two big men in long black raincoats and brimmed hats pushed through the crowd and stood next to them.

Both men had sallow faces and double chins, and one had a black pencil moustache sitting on his upper lip. It looked as if he had just drunk a cup of ink. Amos and Dunc looked at each other with grimaces on their faces.

"They look terrible," Amos whispered.

They moved away from the two men as far as possible. It wasn't too difficult since the rest of the crowd was shying away too. Nobody wanted to stand close to them.

The announcer said Lash's name over the loudspeaker, and Lash stepped behind the gate. The crowd grew quiet, except the men in dark coats. They grumbled something to each other that neither Dunc or Amos could hear.

The starter blew a whistle, and Lash disappeared in a blur, racing down the track. He flipped his board up one side at least fifteen feet in the air, held it above his head with both hands, did a somersault, and landed on his board again.

He did it once more right at the finish line, and instead of landing on his board, he landed on his feet with the board raised over his head.

The crowd went wild.

"That's incredible," Dunc said. "I've never seen anything like that."

"That's because it's never been done before. Lash told me he was going to try it for the first time here—at least, that's what I think he was trying to tell me."

"What's he call it?"

"The Maggie tubular sky-high inverse sub-sub-shakysault."

Dunc frowned. "The only thing I understand is the name of his board—that's Maggie, right?"

"Right. Come on, let's go talk to him."

Lash was standing by the judges' table. He was still wearing his helmet but had taken off his glasses. The skateboard was tucked under his arm. He was being interviewed by Dirk Cordoba, a local television sports announcer. Dunc and Amos stopped and waited for the interview to end.

"Another incredible display of aerial acrobatics," Dirk said. "Lash Malesky, how do you do it?" Dirk wasn't looking at Lash. He was watching the camera. He had a big plastic smile on his face. The microphone was in one hand, and with a finger he flicked a gob of makeup out of the cleft in his chin.

"Awesome, Dirk," Lash said. "It's stoked, smoking to the wall—"

"Isn't that a new board, Lash?" Dirk interrupted. He pointed at the board without taking his eyes off of the camera. "It isn't the same one you used at the Nationals last year, is it?"

"Rad. Barrelling—"

"I noticed it says 'Maggie' across the top." Amos was amazed that Dirk could notice so much without ever taking his eyes off the camera.

"Tweak—"

"Well, thank you very much for your time, Lash," Dirk said. "I wish you the best for the rest of the day and the finals tomorrow."

"Boned—"

"This is Dirk Cordoba with skateboarding ace Lash Malesky. Back to you in the booth, George." He kept smiling until the red light on the top of the camera turned off. The smile went off with the light.

Lash held out his hand to Dirk. "Greased, man . . . too much—"

"Where's the makeup man?" Dirk shouted. He started pacing back and forth in front of the camera. "Did you see that gob of makeup? It left my chin undefined. Where is he?" He hurried off toward the van that was serving as his dressing room while the skateboard championships were going on.

"Nice run, Lash," Amos said.

"A real jam," Lash said. "Like jelly."

"I didn't know boning out would be so painful." Amos shook his head. "I broke a tree with my body."

"Ecological." Lash smiled and patted him on the back.

"So how do you do stunts like that?" Dunc asked. "I've never seen anything like them before."

"Bone out, tweak, and ride the high five."

"What did he say?"

"He said Maggie's a new prototype made by Slapjack Skateboards."

"How did you know that?"

"I don't know. Ever since I hit that tree branch, he's started to make sense to me."

"Doesn't that scare you?"

"It terrifies me."

Lash took his helmet off and shook his hair free. "Next jam."

"What?" Dunc asked.

"He said he'll see us later."

"Oh."

"Later, dude."

"Tomorrow night"—Amos nodded—"after you win the championship. That's all Mom's been able to talk about. She's had me cleaning the house all day. I have to defumigate the chair where Uncle Alfred sits."

Lash laughed.

"It's not funny," Amos said.

"Too radical . . ."

As they watched Lash, the two ugly men pushed their way through the crowd in the direction of the gate. They followed him. The breeze rushed past them right into Amos's and Dunc's faces. They looked at each other and wrinkled their noses.

"Who do you suppose they are?" Amos asked.

"They look like thugs out of an old black and white movie. Something out of the forties."

"Yeah, maybe a horror movie."

"The Stench That Strangled Detroit."

"Exactly."

The men disappeared behind a building.

Amos and Dunc hadn't taken two steps when Lash came running over to them. His eyes were wide and wild. He was panting, too out of breath to say anything.

"What happened?" Dunc asked.

"Crash and burn, crash and burn!"

Amos's eyes popped wide open. "Someone just stole Maggie!"

Chapter 4

They stared at Lash.

"Relax," Dunc said. "We'll find her." He wasn't as sure of himself as he tried to sound.

"Copped, *copped*."

Dunc looked at Amos. "He means stolen," Amos said. "Not lost."

"We'll still find her. You said she disappeared in the bathroom?"

Lash nodded.

"Then let's go check out the bathroom." Dunc led Amos and Lash through the crowd over to a small white brick building. They went in the door marked MEN. There was no one else inside.

"What happened?" Dunc asked. The air was stiff and stale and caught in his nose.

"Like, toilet."

"He says he was using the toilet and a hand came under the door and grabbed the board and it was gone."

"Did they take anything else?"

"That's all he's got," Amos said. "The board and the helmet and his glasses."

"Did you see or hear anything else?"

Lash shook his head.

"What do you suppose happened?" Amos asked. He walked over to the closed door next to the stall Lash had been in. "Could she be in one of the toilets? Does Maggie float, Lash?"

"Be serious, Amos," Dunc said.

"I am serious. Stranger things have happened to us."

"The board didn't fly into a toilet."

"Total—you think—right?"

"I don't know what you mean," Dunc said.

"Have thoughts," Amos said. "Like you think—have thoughts. That's cool, man."

Dunc stared at Amos. "Amos, aren't you getting a little . . . loose?"

Amos had turned to wash his hands. He cut the water off and wiped his hands on his pants. "Places like this make me want to wash over and over. Kind of like bus depot bathrooms."

Dunc walked over to the door. "Let's look for something out here." The fresh wind cleared their nostrils. They couldn't find anyone with a skateboard.

"Now what?" Amos asked.

"I guess we look for clues," Dunc said. "If there was a crime, there must be clues. Amos, you look back in the bathroom. Lash and I will check out the park."

"As long as I don't have to touch that floor. If finding clues means touching that floor, forget it. I'll look for clues on the walls. Maybe there's a few on the ceiling."

"All right. If you find any clues on the floor, leave them. I'll get them later."

Just as Amos reached the bathroom door, a chubby man in a long gray trenchcoat scuttled around the corner. He saw Lash and made a little whistling squeak like the sound of a frightened mouse.

"Where's the skateboard?" he asked.

"Who are you?" Dunc asked.

"I'm Sherman," he said. "Sherman Hemlock—the skateboard company hired me to protect the board." He looked at Lash's empty hands, then around on the ground next to them. "Where's the skateboard?" he repeated.

Lash shrugged his shoulders and sighed and shook his head. "Bummer."

"She's gone," Amos said. "Somebody copped her."

Sherman's face was small and pudgy, and every time he breathed the nostrils on his pug nose flared in and out. "Oh dear, oh dear." He rubbed his hands together and paced back and forth. When he turned around to look at them, his face was redder.

"I was hired to watch that board. That was my only job, just watch the board, and now it's gone. I just went to get some cotton candy, for goodness' sake, and just like that the board is gone. Mother always told me to be an accountant, but no, I wanted the glamour of private investigation, the new Sherlock Holmes, and now I've gone and blown a simple thing like watching a skateboard. What am I going to do? Tell me, what am I going to do?"

"Bummer," Lash said again.

"First of all," Dunc said, "I think you have to calm down."

Sherman stopped pacing and stood in front of them. He was still wringing his hands. "You're right, of course. Give me a moment to get control of myself." He took a deep breath and let it out slowly. When he was finished, some of the redness had gone out of his face.

"Better." He breathed deeply again. "A rational mind requires control. That's the first rule of the art of deduction. Now, what is the first step to take in the case of the missing skateboard?" He took a notebook and pencil out of his pocket, licked the end of the pencil, and looked at the boys. "What are the facts?"

"The facts are what we're trying to find

out," Dunc said. "Maggie disappeared in the bathroom. Lash and I are going to look for clues in the park while Amos tries to find some in there."

"Unless they're on the floor," Amos said. "I don't want any new clues if they're on the bathroom floor. That floor is more disgusting than my uncle Alfred's feet."

"Al-fred," Sherman said, writing furiously in his notebook. "Is that with one *r* or two?"

"One," Amos said.

"Let's get going." Dunc led Lash off into the crowd while Sherman followed Amos into the bathroom.

Chapter 5

"Step back, son," Sherman said. "Let an eye trained in the art of deduction investigate this first." He pushed Amos out of the way.

Sherman walked with his chin out and his hands clasped behind his back, clicking his tongue as he searched. "See this ceiling?" he asked.

"Yeah."

"It's called a dropped ceiling. Remind me to get a ladder and look in the air space above it."

He went into the first stall. "Just as I suspected."

"What?"

"Look at the toilet paper. See how the roll comes over the top instead of down the back?"

"So?"

"So that is a fact, and a fact could be a clue." He wrote something down in his notebook and tapped the side of his head with his pencil. "Remember that."

He stopped by the sink and carefully examined the porcelain. Amos watched him.

"Sherman, I don't see where any of this is getting us."

"That's because you don't have a trained professional mind. I do." He turned on the water and turned it off again. "The spigot," he said as he wrote, "is made of stainless steel, and it does not drip. Hmm." He thought for a moment and shook his head as if he were puzzled. "Kneel down here with me."

"No."

"Then I'll do it alone." Sherman knelt down to examine the drain trap. As he did, something crunched beneath his knee.

"Hello, what's this?" He stood back up again. "It looks like a clue."

"It looks like a peanut. A crushed peanut."

"Pea-nut," Sherman said, writing furiously in his notebook. "Is that p-e-e or p-e-a?"

"On this floor it's probably p-e-e," Amos said. He wiped his hands on his pants. He couldn't stop wiping his hands on his pants.

"P-e-e." Amos could hear Sherman's pencil scribbling.

"Where do you suppose it came from?" Amos asked.

"Use your deductive reasoning. Where do peanuts come from?"

"The store."

"Be more creative. Where do people buy peanuts still in the shell?"

"At the zoo, to feed the elephants."

"A possibility," Sherman said, "though rather a remote one. No, I think a better possibility would be the circus."

"But we haven't had a circus in town for months, and the zoo is just across the street."

"All the more reason to suspect the circus. Always suspect the obvious, son. In this line of work always assume the probable is improbable." He started pacing back and forth in front of the stalls. "Now, circuses always have elephants, right?"

"Right."

"And they always teach circus elephants tricks, right?"

"Right."

Sherman closed his notebook and stuffed it in his pocket with a flourish. He looked at Amos smugly. "Case solved," he said.

"Where's Maggie?"

"On her way to Florida," Sherman said, "for the winter."

"Florida for the winter? You figured that out from a peanut you crushed with your knee?"

"It's a simple case of deduction. The facts: A skateboard is stolen. Peanuts are found at the scene of the crime. The circus sells peanuts and has elephants. Elephants perform tricks. Circuses are on their way to Florida this time of the year for the winter. The deduction: The skateboard was stolen to be a part of an elephant trick in the circus. It is now on its way to Florida. Simple." He strode toward the door.

"Where are you going?"

"To check on plane tickets to Florida. I'll apprehend the villains just as they cross the border. Head them off at the pass, as they say in the movies."

"Don't you think—"

"Why? We don't need to think anymore. The case is solved. You can consider the zoo if you like. I'm off to Florida. Good luck." He bounded out the door and was gone.

Amos was standing in the sun in front of the bathroom when Dunc and Lash came back. "Where's Sherman?" Dunc asked.

"On his way to Florida."

"What?"

"You don't want to hear about it." He looked at them. "What did you guys find out?"

"Wasted," Lash said.

Amos nodded. "Nothing, right? We found a peanut."

"One peanut?" Dunc asked.

"Yeah. Maybe we should check out the

zoo. Maybe the thieves bought the peanuts there."

"You got all that from a peanut? We don't know who stole the board. How will we know them when we see them? Look for somebody with another peanut?"

"Tripping." Lash sighed.

"What else can we do?" Amos asked.

Dunc sighed. "Not much, I guess. Let's go." He started leading them toward the park entrance. He stopped. "Wait a minute."

"What?" Amos bumped into him.

"What about those two guys that smelled so bad?"

"The thugs out of the forties horror movie?"

"Yeah."

"What about them?"

"Didn't they seem a little suspicious to you? I mean, do guys like that spend their Saturdays watching skateboard tournaments?"

"No. Guys like that spend their Saturdays at the rest home kicking the canes out from under old people."

"Dudes." Lash's head bobbed.

"There were two guys in raincoats that watched your run," Amos explained. "You didn't see them because you were busy."

"Rock and roll."

Dunc smiled. "At least now we have suspects. Let's keep our eyes open." He started walking toward the street. "Come on. Let's get over to the zoo."

Chapter · 6

At the zoo entrance they were confronted by a post covered with signs pointing to the different exhibits.

"So what kinds of animals eat peanuts?" Dunc asked.

"Elephants," Amos said. They followed the sign that pointed to the elephant exhibit. "And monkeys."

As they were passing a side trail, Dunc grabbed them both by the shoulders and pulled them behind a tree.

Dunc glanced around the trunk. "Very carefully and very quietly look around the tree toward the elephants." They did. The two thugs were standing in front of the exhibit with their hands in their pockets and their hats pulled down over their foreheads.

"So what?" Amos said. "They don't know who we are."

"They know who Lash is." Dunc peeked around the side of the tree. "Listen to what they have to say. Maybe we can learn something about Maggie."

The men stood like dirty statues, not moving and not saying anything, either. The elephants were all standing at the back of their pen with their trunks curled up.

"Are they dead?"

"Come on, Amos," Dunc said. "Of course they're not dead."

"Then why don't they move?"

"There *is* something about them," Dunc said. "Something funny." He looked at them for a moment. "Look at the back of the one closest to us."

His raincoat had white and green splotches all down the left shoulder and back.

"What does that look like to you?"

"It looks like someone squirted a whole tube of toothpaste down his back," said Amos. "The multicolored kind."

"No." Dunc shook his head. "It looks more like bird droppings, don't you think?"

"Could be. Yeah, wait a minute. That looks like the bottom of the parrot cage at the pet store."

"That's what I was thinking."

"I don't want to get involved with that bird again." There used to be a repulsive old parrot that sat in the window of the pet store. Sometime back, Dunc and Amos had learned that it triggered on swear words. They taped some of the things it said and found out that it knew where there was a treasure.

The treasure turned out to be a sack of wheat, which is a great treasure for a parrot but not of much use to two boys. "That was the most disgusting bird in the world."

"Right, and the color on the thug's coat matches the color of the droppings in the bottom of the parrot cage."

Amos looked around the tree again. The thugs still hadn't moved. "I think you're right," he said. "Maybe they bought the parrot."

"Either that, or they've been wherever the parrot is."

"Do you think Maggie might be at the pet store?"

"I don't know." Dunc shook his head.

"Rad. Gerbils, guinea pigs. Boned."

"No," Amos said. "The animals didn't ride Maggie—"

"Quiet." Dunc nudged his shoulder. "Watch."

As if coming out of a trance, the man with the bird droppings down his back reached into his pocket. He took out a peanut and threw it toward the elephants. One of the larger ones sniffed at it but shook his head and snorted and left it where it lay.

"So now what, Emile?" the other thug asked.

"Now we wait."

"Wait for what?"

"Claude, you were born with oatmeal for brains. We wait for the highest bidder."

"Oh yeah," Claude said, "the highest bidder. Give me a peanut." Emile reached into his pocket, took out a peanut, and handed it to Claude. Claude threw it to the elephants. They all moved away and stared at the peanut on the ground.

"So why do we wait?"

"Claude—"

"No, I mean why don't we find out the skateboard's secret ourselves? If we did, we could make a fortune."

"Because nobody except the designer knows how the skateboard's frictionless bearing works. We might screw it up. If that skateboard is broken, it won't be worth a hundred dollars."

"And what if it isn't broken?"

"It'll be worth a million."

Claude scratched his ear. "Is that more than a hundred?"

Emile slapped Claude on the back of the head. "You're so dumb, Claude. You couldn't pour water out of a boot with the instructions written on the bottom of the heel. One million has lots more zeros than a hundred —it's at least three times as much. Maybe four." He threw another peanut to the elephants. They ignored it.

"A frictionless bearing?" Amos whispered.

"Rad—Maggie!" Lash bounced, and Duncan held him down.

"So that's why you can do that stunt," Dunc said.

"The Maggie sky-high inverse sub-sub-shakysault with mctwist." Amos nodded his head. "It's tubular, man."

Claude pulled on the brim of his hat. "But what if someone finds the skateboard while we're waiting?"

"How could anyone find it? No one would think of looking for it where it's hidden."

"No one would want to find it. I'm even afraid to go there." Claude's shoulders shuddered.

"At least it's safe. Let's go look at the alligators. It's nearly feeding time, and I like to watch them eat—they swallow things whole without puking." They left the elephants and started walking toward the alligator pit. The boys watched them until they were out of sight.

"We can go now." Dunc stepped out from

behind the tree. Amos and Lash followed him.

"Now what?" Amos asked.

"Now we wait by the entrance for them to leave."

"What if they see us?"

"We'll hide. When they come out, we'll follow them to wherever the bird is, and wherever the bird is, Maggie will be."

"I don't know if I want to find Maggie anymore," Amos said.

"Why?"

"Did you see how frightened Claude was? Someone or something must be guarding her. If he's afraid of it, imagine what it could do to us."

"Total bummer."

"He's right, Dunc." Amos nodded. "He says we have to go for it—we do."

"He said all that?"

Amos nodded again.

"In two words?"

"Well. You've kind of got to know how to say the words the right way."

Dunc stared at him for a long time, then nodded slowly. "All right." He paused. Amos was studying him, running his eyes up and down, then doing the same for Lash.

"What are you doing?"

"You two are meatier than me," Amos said. "If this guardian is something that eats meat, I want to be eaten last. Maybe he'll fill up on you guys and leave me alone."

Dunc shook his head and led them to the entrance. "I've got to go get something from home. If they leave before I get back, follow them until they get to wherever they're going, and then one of you come and get me."

"What are you going to get?"

"Just something we might need. I'll be back in a few minutes." He ran across the street to his bike and waved as he rode past them.

Lash and Amos hid in the trees next to the entrance and waited.

Chapter · 7

They were still hiding when Dunc came back with a duffel bag in his hand.

"What did you get?" Amos asked.

"Nothing much. Haven't they come out yet?"

"No. We're still waiting. I hate it when you do that."

"What?"

"Have secrets. Like the duffel bag. I hate that."

"It's all right. You'll find out later."

"I just hate it."

"Thin," Lash said, interrupting. "Air."

"What?" Dunc asked.

Amos turned to Lash. "Yeah. They vanished, didn't they?"

"They'll be out," Dunc said. "This is the only exit." He joined them in the trees.

The sun was beginning to set when Emile and Claude finally left the zoo. The boys waited until they were half a block gone, then followed them. The men led them away from the zoo and down toward the river, the part of town where even bikers didn't go after dark.

The boys stopped when Emile and Claude went into a shabby apartment building. Amos shuddered—the windows, he thought, look like holes in a corpse. *Why would I think that?*

They watched as a light on the third floor came on.

"Bummer."

"Yeah," Amos said. "Me, too—but we have to go in."

"We don't know if she's in there." Dunc rubbed the back of his neck and waited—something he always did when he didn't want to go into a building where the windows looked like holes in a corpse. "Besides, I can't see us blasting by those two guys. What we need to do is get a look in the apartment and see if Maggie is there, or at least find out if they have the parrot. One of us is going to have to go in."

"One of us," Amos said, his voice flat.

"Right."

"You mean Lash."

"No."

"You mean you."

"No."

"Me."

Dunc nodded.

"Bummer." Amos sighed. "That's why you brought the bag, right? You brought a grappling hook, and I'm going to scale the building."

"I couldn't throw a grappling hook that high."

Amos looked up toward the window. "Yeah, it is kind of a long throw. I don't think I could make it, either."

"I didn't bring a grappling hook, Amos."

"Then what did you bring?"

"I figure the only way we can get in the apartment is to be disguised."

"Maybe we could pay someone from off the street to go up there." Amos dug in his pocket. "I've got fifty cents. What do you guys have?"

"You're going up, Amos."

"Please. No. Why?"

"Because you're the only one that can fit in the disguise. Besides, you love acting."

"What do you mean, I love acting?"

"Don't you remember when we were kids playing cowboys and Indians? You used to always be the Indian and run out of the house in your underwear with a feather in your hair."

"Rad." Lash smiled. "Tubular."

Dunc unzipped the bag and took out the costume. It consisted of a robe and a flesh-colored skullcap.

"What disguise is that?"

"A Hare Krishna."

"A hairy Krishna? I don't know a thing about hairy Krishnas."

"They're a religious cult. Go up to the apartment, and try to sell them some flowers or something. Try to find Maggie when they open the door."

"This will never work."

"Sure it will," Dunc said. "You're a tremendous actor."

"How do you know?"

"Because you're tremendous at everything you do."

Amos studied Dunc's face for a long time, then he nodded. "You'd lie to me."

"Not this time."

"Right." But he put the robe and skullcap on. The breeze caught the robe and blew it out away from his body. He look like a badminton birdie standing on end.

"I don't have any flowers."

Dunc moved into a nearby vacant lot and came back with a handful of dandelions. "Here."

Amos took the flowers and started walking up the stairs to the door of the apartment building. "I have a question."

"What?"

"Why do they call themselves hairy Krishnas if they shave all their hair off?"

"I don't know." Dunc pointed at the door. "You're stalling."

Amos sighed, straightened his shoulders, and went into the building.

Chapter · 8

It was dark in the hallway. Amos knocked on the door once and heard Emile and Claude fumbling around inside, but no one opened the door. He knocked again and waited. Something moved in the dark end of the hallway. It could have been a rat. Or a Doberman. Or a Buick. He held his breath.

He heard a latch move, and the door opened. Claude stood in the doorway with his hands on his hips. He was frowning. He still had his raincoat on, and Amos couldn't see past him.

"What do you want?"

"Hairy Krishna," Amos said. "I represent the Church of . . . of . . ."

"The Church of what?"

"The Church of the Holy Disemboweled." He shifted his feet. The toes of his cross trainers stuck out from beneath the robe.

"What do you want?"

"I want to know if you'd make a contribution to our church. It would go for a worthy cause."

"I don't give my money away. I don't do anything nice."

"But you won't be giving your money away. You'd receive these beautiful flowers along with our appreciation."

"Those look like dandelions."

"Sure, they look like dandelions, but they're not. They're special flowers from the mountains in India. They're magical."

"Magical?" Claude scratched his chin, then looked over his shoulder. "Emile, do you want to buy some magical flowers?"

Emile's head appeared over Claude's shoulder. "They look like dandelions."

"That's what I said. What do you mean, magical?"

"These flowers are guaranteed to freshen your apartment forever, and you don't even need to add water. Let me show you." He ducked between Claude's legs into the room. It was dank and darker than the hallway, and it took a moment before he could see well enough to look for Maggie or the parrot. They weren't there, and he turned to leave.

Emile and Claude were blocking the door.

"See?" Amos smiled. A tiny smile. "It smells fresher in here already."

"It doesn't smell any different to me." Claude eyed Amos suspiciously. "Who are you, really, and what do you want?"

"I'm—I'm—"

"What church did you say you were representing?"

"Church? Did I say church?"

Claude took a step toward him. His hands were clenched into fists the size of bowling balls.

"The Church of the Holy Disemboweled," Emile cut in. "Don't be a dummy, Claude. Just take a whiff. I think they do make a difference." He reached into his pocket. "I'll give you a dime for them flowers."

"A whole dime?"

"What, that's not a good price?"

"Well—"

"You're right. Do you have change? Two nickels for a dime?"

"No."

"I'll tell you what. I'll give you a dime now, and you bring up another bunch of those flowers later."

"All right." He stepped toward the door. Emile stepped aside, but Claude wouldn't move.

"Why are you in such a hurry? Don't you like our company?"

"Sure I do, it's just that I have to—have to . . ."

"Have to what?"

"Shave my head. It's getting a little stubbly." He rubbed the top of the skullcap.

"Let him by, Claude," Emile said. He pushed Claude to the side. "If he wants to leave and shave his head, let him leave and shave his head. Don't interfere with other people's religious beliefs." He let Amos squeeze out the doorway. " 'Bye."

" 'Bye. Hairy Krishna."

"You too." He shut the door.

Amos ran down the stairs and out the door. Dunc and Lash were waiting for him.

"They didn't have the parrot or Maggie," he said. "Now what do we do?"

"The pet store," Dunc said. "We'll try the pet store in the morning."

Chapter • 9

The pet store had just opened when they arrived. The parrot wasn't in the window.

"Can I help you?" The store owner stepped from behind the counter and looked at them.

"We were wondering what happened to the old parrot you used to keep in the window. Did it die?"

"No, it didn't die. It—wait a minute. I remember you two. You're the ones who tape-recorded my parrot. You made him talk for hours. The poor thing had laryngitis for a week."

"That's us," Dunc said. "Is he all right?"

"I think his throat was sore—he kept asking for mouthwash and repeating a phrase I learned in the navy. Other than that, he was fine."

"Where is he?" Dunc asked.

"I sold him to the zoo a month ago. He's in the new tropical bird and monkey exhibit." The store owner busied himself straightening the shelf of kitty litter. He was obviously in a hurry for the boys to leave.

"Thanks," Dunc said.

"Don't mention it." He looked down his nose at the boys. "You're not going to tape any of my other birds, are you?"

"No."

"Good."

"So long." They left the store.

"Pets. Tripper." Lash waved as they walked out.

"So now we go back to the zoo?" Amos asked.

"Where else?" Dunc nodded. "It figures with all those bird droppings on his coat that they were from the bird house at the zoo, doesn't it?"

"Rad." Lash nodded. "Droppings."

"The zoo," Amos repeated. "Where the monster that eats meat is waiting."

"We don't know that," Dunc said, starting off in the direction of the zoo. "Not for sure."

"I do."

"Meat," Lash said. "Total."

"No," Amos said, his voice sharp. "When it's your meat, it isn't total."

"Rad."

Chapter 10

At the zoo they looked for the bird and monkey exhibit, and they found it in a matter of minutes. They came to a large cage full of trees so thick, they couldn't see the far side. It was also filled with the music of singing birds, and monkeys were climbing through the branches and over rocks on the ground, squawking at each other. There was a large pile of rocks in the back with a small cave in the side.

A big chimpanzee was sitting at the cave entrance scratching its armpit. It looked at Amos and puckered its lips.

"There it is," Dunc said. He pointed to one of the trees in the front. The old parrot was sitting on a branch with its eyes closed, not moving. As they watched, it opened one eye, looked at them, belched, and went to the bathroom all over a baboon that was sitting underneath it. The baboon screamed, and the parrot mimicked it.

"Now it swears in baboonese too," Amos said. "Can I borrow your helmet and glasses, Lash?"

"Rad." Lash handed the helmet and glasses to Amos.

Dunc watched. "What do you need those for?"

"If we're going to be anywhere close to that bird, I want to have as much of my body covered as possible."

"Come on, Amos—there's nothing to worry about."

"Right." Amos snorted. "Tell that to the baboon."

The parrot looked at them but didn't say anything.

"Bird," Lash said. "Awesome."

"You should hear it talk," Amos said.

"You wouldn't believe some of the things it can say."

"Ear me."

Amos whispered something in his ear.

"Rad." Lash smiled. "Body parts."

Dunc peered through the bars. "I don't see Maggie anywhere," he said.

"Bummer."

"You guys be careful," Amos said.

Dunc looked over his shoulder. "Be careful about what?"

Amos pointed at the parrot. It was standing on one foot and eyeing them intently.

"He can't hit us from there."

"I wouldn't bet on that."

"All right," Dunc said, "Emile and Claude must have gone into the cage." He moved to the cage door and tried to open it. It was locked.

"Do you suppose they have a key?" Amos asked.

"They might," Dunc said, "but it seems to me the zoo keepers would keep a pretty tight hold on cage keys. They wouldn't want just anyone going into the lion cage."

"They must wait until the door's unlocked," Amos said.

Dunc looked into the keyhole. "When would that be?"

"When they feed the animals," Amos said. "They usually feed them in the evenings and mornings."

Dunc walked back from the cage and stepped into the bushes on the far side of the walk. "Let's wait in here."

"Why?"

"If the only time Emile and Claude can get in the cage is when the animals are being fed, they might show up now."

"Good idea." Amos and Lash joined him.

They hid themselves just in time. In a few moments they heard the screech of wheels badly in need of oiling, and they saw an old man with a big gray moustache pushing a cart loaded with every kind of animal food in the world. He was singing loudly and so badly out of tune, it almost screeched.

"It's making my teeth loose," Amos said.

"Be quiet." Dunc poked him.

The old man stopped in front of the bird

and monkey exhibit. The animals started hopping up and down and chattering excitedly.

"Calm down," the old man said. "It's not like you haven't eaten for a week. And quit jabbering so loudly. I'm not completely deaf."

He took a key out of his pocket and unlocked the door, but he held back and didn't open it.

"Here, Kissing Gertie." From the top of the cart he took a banana and threw it through the bars. It landed in front of the pile of rocks. The big chimpanzee smiled, picked up the banana, and began eating it, smacking its lips. With its mouth full of banana it looked to where Amos was hiding and smiled again. Crushed banana goo squeezed out between its yellow teeth. The man opened the door and pushed the cart through. Shutting the door, he moved toward the back of the exhibit. All the animals except the parrot and Gertie followed him. Soon they were all lost in the trees. The old man had left the door unlocked.

"Let's go," Dunc said. He stepped out of the bushes.

As they went into the cage, Amos looked at the parrot. It was watching him with a funny look his face. *He's smiling,* Amos thought—*he's giving me a parrot smile.* He pulled Lash's helmet tight down on his head, adjusted the sunglasses, and followed Dunc and Lash into the cage.

Chapter 11

"Maggie must be in that little cave," Dunc said, pointing. Amos followed his finger. The chimpanzee had disappeared, leaving half its banana by the cave entrance.

"Where's Gertie?" he asked.

"She must have gone with the other animals. Come on." He led the way back toward the cave.

There was a sudden guttural scream out of the trees behind them, and Amos jumped at least four feet in the air. He turned around just in time to see a huge furry creature with arms that looked a mile long leap out of a tree and grab him.

Whummmph!

The creature's face was only an inch from his. It pulled its lips back to reveal long yellow teeth. He managed one short scream as the mouth came toward him for what he was sure would be the kill.

"Ah-hmmph." His voice was muffled by loud smacking sounds as the creature wrapped its leathery lips around his face. He tore his mouth free for a quick gulp of air and a cry.

"It's Kissing Gertie! Help mmph—"

Dunc and Lash turned around. Amos was lying on the ground. Gertie had her arms wrapped around his shoulders and her legs wrapped around his waist. She looked as if she had about half of Amos's skull down her throat. They tried to pull her off, but her arms were like iron. Dunc shook his head. "So this is the monster guarding the skateboard."

"Rad," Lash said. "Gross. Rad. Puke."

"Help. . . ."

"Good job, Amos," Dunc said. "She's not really hurting you. Keep her busy while we look for the board."

Amos managed to pull his mouth away from Gertie's puckered lips. "Don't just stand there, help mmph—" Gertie gave him a wet one.

Dunc watched Amos spit a chunk of prechewed banana out of his mouth.

"I don't know how much time we have," Dunc said.

"Dunc—" Amos fought to get his head clear.

"What?"

"I'm going to kill you. I'm going to kill you bad."

"Pretend she's Melissa."

Amos tried to say something more, but Gertie's lips muffled his reply. Dunc and Lash went into the cave.

There was a sharp turn right after the entrance, and just out of sight was a barred door blocking off a little room. Dunc tried the door and found it unlocked. They went into the room. Maggie was on the floor.

"Awesome." Lash ran and picked up the board and held it in his arms.

"We have to get out of here," Dunc said.

"Jam." He followed Dunc out of the cave.

Amos was still on the ground with Gertie on top of him. He was fighting her off, but his movements were getting weaker.

Lash waved as they went by. “Rad.”

“We have to help him.” Dunc stopped. He looked down and saw the half-eaten banana the zookeeper had thrown to her earlier. He picked it up and threw toward Gertie. She climbed off of Amos and chased down the banana.

Amos groaned and rose slowly to his feet. The sunglasses were sucked halfway off his face, and his eyes looked glazed behind them.

“Are you all right?” Dunc asked.

Amos leaned over with his hands on his knees and shook his head. When he straightened up, his eyes were clearer.

“Never,” he said, “kiss a monkey.”

“Let’s get going.” Dunc took a step toward Amos, then stepped back again. “Whew, Amos. Don’t get too close. You smell something awful.”

“I know, I know,” Amos said, “just like Emile and Claude, or like Uncle Alfred’s socks.”

Dunc grimaced. "Even worse."

Gertie had finished her banana. She looked at Amos and smiled coyly.

"We better get out of here," Amos said. "Now. I don't want to go through that again."

"And if Emile and Claude catch us here," Dunc said, "we're—"

"You're what?" A man's voice stopped them.

The boys turned. Emile and Claude were standing in the cage door, watching them.

Chapter 12

The men stood in the doorway with their hands on their hips. Emile was in front, and he smiled.

"Ah, so what is this?" Emile said. "A rescue party for a skateboard?" He chuckled.

"I think the rescue party is going to need a rescue party," Claude said. He smiled and pushed the sleeves of his raincoat up forearms that looked like raw hams. They stepped forward.

"Get back, get back, you mangy animals!"

Emile and Claude looked over the three

boys' shoulders. Amos, Dunc, and Lash turned around. The old zookeeper was trotting up from the rear of the exhibit, desperately throwing bananas over his shoulder as he went. A crowd of monkeys was chasing him, grabbing the bananas before they could reach the ground.

"I tell ya," the old man said, "I give you monkeys one banana, and you take two. I give you two bananas, and you take three. When's it going to end? This is blackmail, you know." He looked up, saw the crowd of humans in the exhibit, and stopped. "Oh, hello," he said.

"So now we have another member of the party," Claude said. "No matter."

Just at that moment the parrot, sitting on a tree branch directly above Claude, looked over its shoulder, belched once for luck, aimed carefully, and let loose.

Emile turned around to see what his partner was cursing about. A happy scream came from the tree branches, and Kissing Gertie exploded out of the brush. She grabbed Emile. Hard.

"Not again, you hmmph—" Emile said as

he fell backward. The parrot sat above them on the tree branch, nodding its head up and down, laughing.

"Run!" Dunc shouted. They dodged past the cursing thugs and ran toward the zoo entrance. As Lash went past Emile, he broke loose from Gertie and made a grab that knocked the skateboard loose. It flew through the air, and Amos caught it. They skipped left and right through people coming to see the animals, and the last thing Amos saw of the other two boys was when Dunc yelled:

"Get over to the skateboard championships and get lost in the crowd. We'll try to find the police." Then a tour group cut them off, and Amos was alone. He headed across the street toward the skateboard park.

Just before he ducked into the mass of people, he glanced over his shoulder and saw Emile and Claude leaving the zoo, one wiping green stuff out of his eyes and the other wiping monkey slobber off his face. They looked toward the park and saw him and immediately came running across the street.

Amos darted back and forth through the crowd. Emile and Claude were gaining on him. He put on a burst of speed, jumped through the last of the spectators, and suddenly found himself trapped between the thugs and the steep concrete drop of the track.

"Give us the board, Mr. Hare Krishna."

Amos turned. They were walking slowly toward him, evil grins on their faces. He felt the weight of Maggie in his hands and took a deep breath. Just as they reached him, Amos put Maggie down, stepped on it, and pushed out onto the track.

He couldn't remember much of what happened after that. There were vague pictures, mind-photos, but things moved so fast he could never be sure. He remembered going down the track somewhere near the speed of light, and then he thought he might have hit the side and done a flip almost the same as the day before, but higher.

Much higher.

He shot into the air as if he had been fired out of a cannon. Halfway through his trajectory he looked down and saw the track. It seemed to be a skinny white snake across the park, and the people like ants looking up at him. Next to his ear he thought he heard a migrating goose honk. *I'll have to be careful,* he thought—*there are planes up here.* He thought he could see Melissa in the bleachers, but her face was so tiny, he couldn't be sure.

Then it was time to come down.

Bummer, he thought.

As he plummeted to the earth, he thought he heard the announcer say something about a world record. He didn't have time to think about it. He barely had enough time to get Maggie under his feet again before he hit the track.

His agility amazed him. He thought he would just end up as a greasy spot on the concrete, but by some miracle he stayed upright, streaked to the end of the track, and shot over the judges' table.

Oh great, he thought—*the trees.* He covered his stomach with both hands and waited to hit, but he didn't have to worry.

He went too high to hit the trees.

I'm leaving, he thought—*leaving earth.*

I'll never see it again. Not any of it. Not Dunc or Melissa or anybody. He even had time to feel sorry for himself and started to compose a will. *I'll leave Uncle Alfred some new socks, clean ones, and my bike to Dunc and a disease for my sister. . . .*

All that time to think. And the final thought, just as he started back down, was: *I bet I go down faster than I came up.*

But it seemed to go slowly. At least at first. On the way back to earth again, he looked over his shoulder and saw Emile and Claude still waiting for him. He also saw Sherman Hemlock walking through the crowd—he was wearing shorts and a loud flowered shirt and sunglasses and zinc paste on his nose and the tops of his ears. He saw Dunc. And Melissa. There she was, watching him, actually looking right at him.

Then he saw the ground.

It was hurtling up at him at a terrible speed. He had cleared the parking lot and was over the public swimming pool. *Luck,* he thought—*I'm finally getting lucky. I'm going to hit the pool.*

He almost smiled. He plugged his nose

and closed his eyes and prepared to hit the water.

He missed.

He didn't miss by much, only three feet, but he found that the ground is just as hard three feet away from a pool as it is a hundred miles from a pool.

There wasn't any pain. Not at first. He went into the dirt like a bullet—in the exact center of a small decorative flower bed next to the lifeguard chair. The ground, as ground goes, was soft, at least it was before he hit it. But his body packed it, and he tried to remember what his science teacher had told him about the formation of sedimentary rock. He also tried to remember his name. And how to add. None of it worked. *I am,* he thought, *I am. . . .*

"Amazing."

"Huh?" He looked up. Dirk Cordoba was standing over him, shoving a microphone in his face.

"Incredible," Dirk said. "A run of astronomical proportions. If I hadn't seen it, I wouldn't have believed it. Lash, how did you do it?" Amos was still wearing Lash's helmet and glasses.

I am Lash, Amos thought. *My name is Lash. This man is calling me Lash.*

"Tubular," Amos said. "Like rad to the max. I was fully tweaked and boned out and rockin' and rollin'—" He stopped as memory came back. *I'm not Lash. I'm Amos. Amos Bender. No. Amos Binder. And I want my mother. Now.*

"I'm not—"

"You're not," Dirk said, smiling. "Listen, ladies and gentleman, to this boy's modesty. You are, Lash, there is no question that you are."

"Are what?"

"You are the greatest skateboarder who has ever lived."

"But—"

"No buts, Lash. No need for any qualifying statements. Your actions speak for themselves. Do you have anything to say?"

"But—"

"Well, thank you, Lash. Thank you for your time. Thank you for this breathtaking run, this moment in history you've given us.

You've left even me speechless. Now back to George in the booth." Before Amos could say anything else, the camera was off and Dirk was on his way to his dressing room.

Chapter · 13

Amos was still on his knees when Dunc and Lash came to him. Lash held Maggie, and Dunc leaned over Amos.

"What happened?" Dunc asked.

"I set a world's record."

"How did you do that?"

"I have no idea, but I don't want to do it again. Can you help me with these—my arms won't bend." Dunc took the helmet and glasses off and gave them to Lash.

"I saw Claude and Emile and Sherman," Amos said. "What happened to them?"

Dunc smiled. "Either Sherman used karate, like he said, or he bent over to pick up his notebook and fell on them, like I think—either way, he knocked them down into the track, and the cops caught them."

"Did you tell the police what happened?"

"No. Sherman's telling them about how he used karate to apprehend the circus thieves. He started talking before we had a chance."

"And they believe that?"

"Well. Enough, anyway."

"We better go straighten them out." He took two steps before Dunc stopped him.

"Don't bother. They won't believe you."

"Why not?"

"Because Sherman has the notes to back up what he says."

Amos groaned. "Oh, well. Maybe it's not a total loss. I think I saw Melissa in the stands when I was riding Maggie. I figure this is it—world record, hero. She *has* to be impressed with me now. Let's go talk to her."

"Like," Lash said, "thanks."

"Lash," Dunc said. "You actually said a

sentence. Sort of—well, two words that work, anyway."

Lash nodded. "Tubular."

"See you tonight at dinner." Amos smiled.

Lash walked off through the crowd that was just beginning to gather with Maggie in one hand and his helmet and glasses in the other. Everyone began cheering.

"Oh." Dunc stopped. "I don't think it will do much good to talk to Melissa. I just saw her. She was on her way over here, but she stopped when she met Lash—I think she thinks he made the run. Not you."

"Great. That's just great." Amos leaned over and tried to pick some of the grass out of the knees of his pants. His fingers still didn't work. "It's just not fair."

"What's not fair?"

"The whole silly mess. We do all the work saving Maggie, and Sherman gets all the credit. I make the skateboard run of a lifetime, and the whole world and Melissa think Lash made it because I was wearing his helmet and glasses."

"The problem has nothing to do with fairness."

"What's the problem, then?"

"The problem is," Dunc said, "that you have the worst luck in the world." Dunc put his arm around his friend. "C'mon. We have to get you cleaned up. There's a big dinner at your house tonight."

"Why get cleaned up?"

"Because you stink to high heaven."

"So? Everybody will think it's Uncle Alfred's feet. He has the smelliest feet in the world. And he picks at them."

"Through his socks. I know."

"Right after dinner, while he's watching the television with Dad. It'll make you sick."

"I know, I know. Let's go."

"But it's really disgusting. You should see it."

"If I come over tonight, I will."

"If? What do you mean, if? You have to come. After what I went through today, I couldn't put up with Alfred without you. It wasn't good, Dunc—none of this. I went really high and there were geese and planes and I almost got a nosebleed and then I started down and I had time to compose my will and I was so scared I wanted my mother and—"

"It's all right, Amos." Dunc took his hand and led him. The arm still wouldn't bend, and Amos walked like Frankenstein. "It's going to be all right."

"Really?"

"Sure." Dunc nodded, lying only a little. "Everything will be all right. . . ."

Be sure to join Dunc and Amos in these other Culpepper Adventures:

The Case of the Dirty Bird

When Dunc Culpepper and his best friend, Amos Binder, first see the parrot in a pet store, they're not impressed—it's smelly, scruffy, and missing half its feathers. They're only slightly impressed when they learn that the parrot speaks four languages, has outlived ten of its owners, and is probably 150 years old. But when the bird starts mouthing off about buried treasure, Dunc and Amos get pretty excited—let the amateur sleuthing begin!

Dunc's Doll

Dunc and his accident-prone friend, Amos, are up to their old sleuthing habits once again. This time they're after a band of doll thieves! When a doll that once belonged to Charles Dickens's daughter is stolen from an exhibition at the local mall, the two boys put on their detective gear and do some serious snooping. Will a vicious watchdog keep them from retrieving the valuable missing doll?

Culpepper's Cannon

Dunc and Amos are researching the Civil War cannon that stands in the town square when they find a note inside telling them about a time portal. Entering it through the dressing room of La Petite, a women's clothing store, the boys find themselves in downtown Chatham on March 8, 1862—the day before the historic clash between the *Monitor* and the *Merrimac.* But the Confederate soldiers they meet mistake them for Yankee spies. Will they make it back to the future in one piece?

Dunc's Halloween

Dunc and his best friend, Amos, are planning the best route to get the most candy on Halloween. But their plans change when Amos is slightly bitten by a werewolf. He begins scratching himself and chasing UPS trucks: he's become a werepuppy!